Snow White's Secret

By Melissa Lagonegro

Illustrated by Artful Doodlers

Random House 🏠 **New York**

Library of Congress Control Number: 2004093748   ISBN: 0-7364-2326-5

www.randomhouse.com/kids/disney

MANUFACTURED IN CHINA

10 9 8 7 6 5 4 3 2

$\mathcal{I}$ have a secret, but you must promise not to tell anyone. Since I've been married to the Prince, I don't get to visit the Dwarfs very often. We always had such fun together, and they enjoyed having my help around the cottage.

But here's my secret—I still help the Dwarfs. They just don't know it.

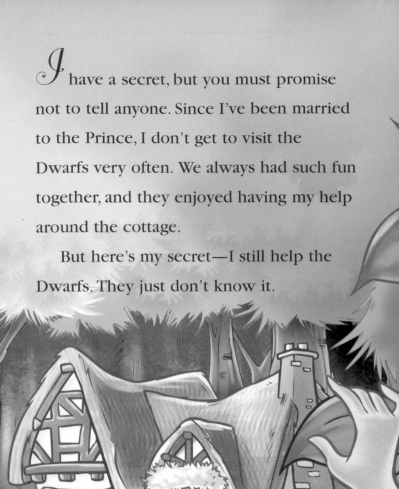

Every once in a while, I sneak off to the Dwarfs' little cottage in the woods. I hide and wait for them to leave for the mines. It's such fun knowing that the Dwarfs will have a clean and cozy cottage to come home to when I'm finished.

As soon as the Dwarfs are out of sight,
my little bluebird friend sings a sweet tune.
Then I sneak into the cottage and get started.

I wouldn't get anything done without my animal friends. They help me tidy up, and they're very good at keeping a secret.

There's a lot of work to do if I want the
cottage to look its best! But first I open all
the windows. The cool forest breeze always
makes the cottage smell fresh and clean.

Then we get right to work! I sweep the floors while the squirrels dust the shelves and the birds remove the cobwebs. The chipmunks and the deer wash and dry the dishes.

When the cottage is clean from top to bottom, I add the finishing touches—that's always my favorite part. I go into the woods and search for the most beautiful flowers. Sometimes I pick daisies, and other times I pick lilies. Flowers always make the cottage look and smell wonderful.

But the Dwarfs' special surprise wouldn't
be complete without some tasty snacks.
I gather lots of fruits, nuts, and berries in the
forest and leave them for the Dwarfs to enjoy.
They especially love gooseberries. Dopey can
eat a whole basketful by himself!

When the little bluebird sings his sweet
song, I must quickly finish my work—the
Dwarfs are on their way home, and I don't
want to be seen.

I hide beside the cottage and wait for them to enter. I love watching their reactions when they see their special surprise.

I try very hard to keep my visits a secret.
But once, I took off my necklace so it
wouldn't get dirty—and I left it on the
kitchen table! Luckily, a squirrel snatched it
back for me before the Dwarfs got home.

Another time, when the Dwarfs
returned home, Happy had an especially
big smile on his face. Doc thought Happy
had sneaked away from the mines during
lunch to clean up the cottage.

Dopey thought Sneezy had done all
the cleaning and dusting, because he was
extra sneezy.

Bashful just knew it had to be Sleepy,
because he was especially tired.

Each Dwarf thought another Dwarf had made
the cottage so lovely. No one suspected me!

For a while, the Dwarfs thought that the forest animals fixed up their cottage. If they only knew that the animals had a lot of help—from me, of course! But I'll never tell the Dwarfs, because it's such fun keeping it a secret.

Now, my secret is just between you, my animal friends, and me. Don't tell anyone—especially the Dwarfs!